Caterpillars Can't Talk

A CHILDREN'S STORY ABOUT LOVE, LOSS AND TRANSFORMATION

KRIS FENTON SIWEK

PUBLISHED WITH LOVE BY KRIS'S DAUGHTER,
STACEY SIWEK SASSINE

Caterpillars Can't Talk: A Children's Story About Love, Loss and Transformation

Published by Wish Flower Press, the children's book imprint
of Silver Tree Publishing, Kenosha, WI.
www.WishFlowerPress.com

Based on the original 1982 story, *What You Are Never Stops*, by Kris Fenton Siwek,
for which her daughter Stacey Siwek Sassine is the copyright holder.

Editing by:
Stacey Siwek Sassine and Kate Colbert

Illustrations by Rich Lo, with inspiration from author Kris Fenton Siwek's original artwork.

Layout and typesetting by:
Courtney Hudson

First edition, May 2020

Hardcover ISBN: 978-1-948238-31-1
Softcover ISBN: 978-1-948238-33-5

Library of Congress Control Number: 2020904022

Created in the United States of America

To Roger and Chad,
with Love

Andy was hurt again. Without a thought, he walked into the woods behind his house. He did not skin his knee or bump his head. Andy had a different kind of hurt.

Andy's dad had died.

Andy sat down by a tree and picked up a leaf that had settled down beside him.

“Hey, I was going to eat that!”

Andy looked down.

“I’m down here, little boy,” the same voice called out again.

Andy looked down. A striped caterpillar was reaching up toward him. Andy knew that caterpillars could not talk, but he leaned over anyway.

"I'm sorry," Andy said. "I didn't see you." He laid the leaf back down by the caterpillar.

"Oh, that's okay. I know that I'm rather small," he giggled. "My name is Clyde."

"Caterpillars can't talk," Andy answered.

"Well, we can pretend for a while, can't we?" asked the caterpillar. Clyde began to nibble on the leaf.

"Yeah, I guess so," Andy laughed. "I'm Andy."

Suddenly, Andy stopped smiling.

"You seem to be very sad about something," said Clyde. He curled his long body around the stem of another leaf and took a big bite.

"I am," Andy replied. "My dad died, and I don't like it at all."

Clyde frowned.

"I know," he said. "I'm sad about that too. I used to see your father here in the woods."

"You did?" Andy asked. "Did he ever talk to you?"

Clyde chuckled.

"Remember, caterpillars can't talk," he replied.

Andy nodded.

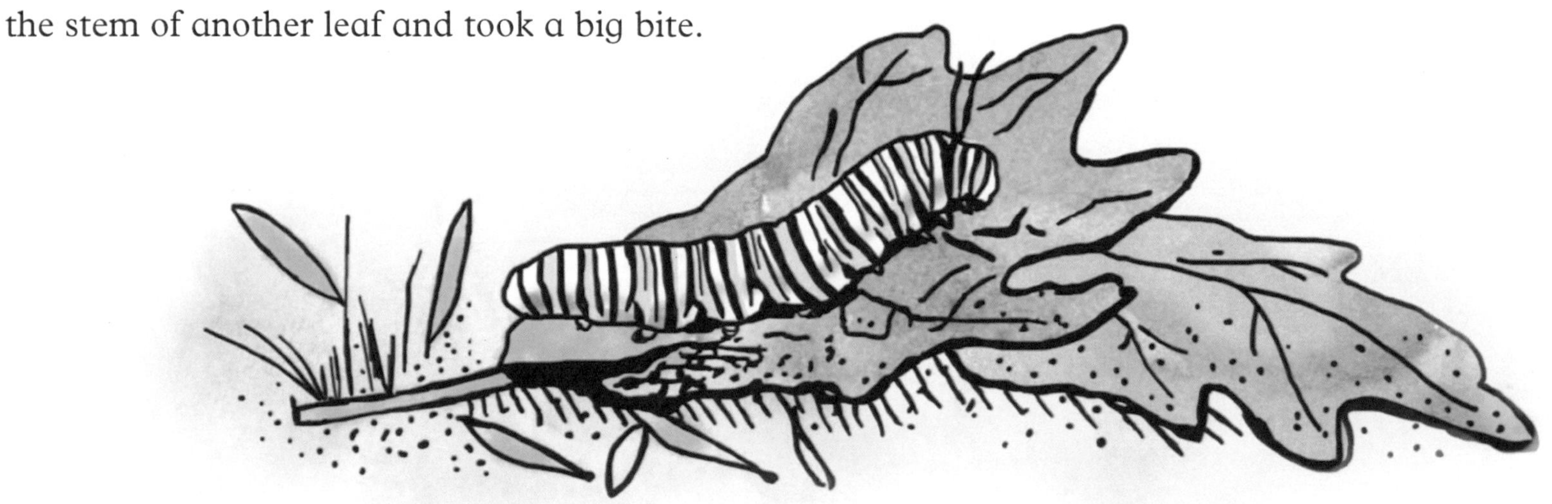

"He seemed like a very nice father," Clyde said.

"Then why did he leave me?" asked Andy.

"Oh, it wasn't his idea. Everybody dies
someday and your father died now."

"It's not fair," Andy sighed. "I loved him."

"He loved you too. And he still does. He is no longer with you,
but that doesn't mean he no longer loves you. He did not die on
purpose." Clyde hesitated. "Did you know that God made this world
as a stopping place where people get ready for a better world?"

"I guess," Andy answered.

"First, people must learn how to live in this world
in order to fit into the next one," said Clyde.

"But I need him," Andy insisted.

"Yes, I know. You will never stop needing or
wanting him," Clyde told him.

"Then why can't he come back to me?" asked Andy.

"This cannot happen," said Clyde. "And people must accept
this, although they will feel hurt and lonely, like you do."

Andy thought about his mother.

“My mom says she needs me, and everyone says I’ve got to take my dad’s place. It’s so hard,” Andy tightened his fists.

“Your father wouldn’t want you to take his place,” Clyde assured him. “He just wants you and your mother to love each other and continue to love him. Just be yourself and, by being yourself, your father will always be a part of you.”

Andy sighed with relief. He knew he was too small to be just like his dad. He had too much growing up to do.

Andy looked down. He pushed his sneaker into the dry ground and kicked up a cloud of dirt. It settled down on Clyde.

"Hey, watch it, Andy!" Clyde shouted angrily. He shook the dirt off his plump little body.

"See?" Andy pouted. "Sometimes I get so mad that I … I …" He paused. Suddenly he felt afraid. "Do you think that God took him away from me because I was bad?"

Andy began to cry.

"Absolutely not! God wouldn't do that to you. He loves all his creations. Cry or get angry if you want to. You have a right. You have lost your father, and it hurts a lot." Clyde crawled closer to Andy.

"You're just a little boy," he whispered.

Andy was certain that he saw tears in Clyde's eyes.

"But if caterpillars can't talk, then they certainly can't cry," he thought.

"And what about my mother? Will she die too?" Andy asked sadly. He scooted down on his back and looked up at the blue sky.

"No. Just because your father died doesn't mean that your mother will die too. She will probably live for a long, long time. But remember, Andy, everybody dies someday. It's not a bad thing. When people die, they enter a new and different life."

Andy listened thoughtfully.

"Did you know that your father is still your father?" Clyde asked. "Although he isn't with you and your mother anymore, this does not change who your father was. People have what is called a soul. Inside of your father was his soul and that soul will never die. You have a soul too. Everybody does."

Andy's eyes widened.

"What you are never stops," said Clyde.

"I don't really understand that, but I do know that my dad is with God," Andy answered. "Sometimes I wish that I could be with him."

Clyde frowned.

"As much as you love your father, please never wish to die. Your father would want you to be happy. Instead, have your father live on through you."

Andy sat up again. He watched as Clyde rubbed his wiggly back against a freshly fallen leaf.

"You know," Clyde said, "caterpillars go through a change in life too. It is called metamorphosis. Something very beautiful happens to us then. It is a kind of death, where we change and begin a new life."

"Death is not beautiful to me," Andy said. "It hurts me too much."

"Yes. The hurt will always be there, Andy. It will take a long time to get over your unhappy feelings about your father's death. You will always miss him. But your father is not unhappy for himself. Life with God is not unhappy."

"I want my dad to hold me again," Andy whispered.

"Hold on to the moments you had. They are special," Clyde answered.

The sun was disappearing behind the trees and the forest was getting dark.

"I guess that I should go home now," Andy said reluctantly. As he got up, he gently stroked Clyde's back. It tickled.

"I liked talking to you," he added, "even though caterpillars can't talk." He smiled.

Clyde nodded as he nibbled on another leaf.

"Look for me tomorrow!" Clyde called out.

"I will," Andy promised, waving as he left.

That evening, Clyde ate and ate until he was big and fat. He crawled to a quiet hiding place and built a small house around himself. This was his cocoon.

The next day, Andy rushed into the woods, looking for Clyde. He could not find him. He visited the woods many times, but he still could not find Clyde.

Finally, he stopped looking.

It was almost summer now. Andy still missed his dad very much. He walked back into the woods behind his house. He sat down by the tree where he and Clyde had met. He remembered the nice time they had together.

Andy thought about his dad. He thought about Clyde. He began to cry.

“Hey, Andy,” said a little voice.

Andy looked around and then down, half-expecting to see his caterpillar friend once again.

“I’m up here,” the voice called out again.

Andy looked up into the trees above him. A beautiful butterfly sat proudly on a low branch. He fluttered down to Andy and rested lightly upon his shoulder. Andy turned his head.

“Remember me?” the butterfly asked softly.

“You’re a butterfly,” Andy said shyly. “And butterflies can’t talk.”

“I’m Clyde,” the butterfly replied, and giggled at their joke.

“Where have you been?” Andy asked. He wiped the tears from his face.

“I had to build my cocoon. Once inside, I took a little rest and my body transformed into a beautiful butterfly,” Clyde answered.

“You are beautiful,” Andy added with a smile.

“Thank you,” Clyde blushed. “And as caterpillars have a new and beautiful life, so do all people, someday … and your father now.” Clyde flew off from Andy’s shoulder and into the air above him.

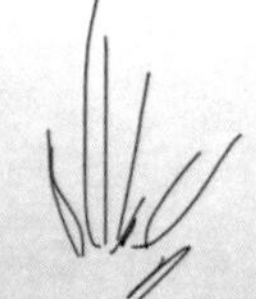

"I must leave you now, Andy," Clyde said, "but I will always remember you."

Andy stood up as Clyde flew past the trees into the blue sky, where he joined what looked like a million butterflies as beautiful as he.

As he watched Clyde disappear from sight, Andy called out softly, "Daddy, I love you."

DECADES IN THE MAKING, A STORY TO SOOTHE BROKEN HEARTS

ABOUT KRIS FENTON SIWEK

Kris Fenton Siwek was a wife, mother of two, fine artist and author. After a dear family friend died suddenly, Kris struggled to find words to comfort his 6-year-old son and help him process his dad's death. She wrote and illustrated a book titled *What You Are Never Stops* and dreamed of publishing the book to help children around the world come to terms with the death of a close loved one.

Sadly, before she could publish the book, Kris herself passed away at the young age of 42, leaving behind two teenaged children who were burdened by the same loss she so eloquently wrote about in her book. After years of struggling to find purpose in her grief, Kris's daughter, Stacey, finally brought the book to life and *Caterpillars Can't Talk: A Children's Story about Love Loss and Transformation* was lovingly published.

Kris Fenton Siwek with her children, Stacey and Jim, on the shores of Lake Michigan, circa 1979.

ABOUT STACEY SIWEK SASSINE

Stacey lives in Cary, Illinois, with her husband and three teenaged daughters. After years of struggling to find purpose surrounding the death of her own mother — the author and illustrator of this beautiful book — Stacey founded One Million Monarchs, a not-for-profit organization with a mission to bring comfort, safety and peace to teenagers and their families who are grieving the loss of a parent, sibling or close friend. With the vision that "We Grow Through What We Go Through," Stacey's goal is to help teens stay on track toward their personal goals after a profound grief experience. After all, "What You Are Never Stops."

Mother and daughter, Kris and Stacey Siwek, circa 1981 at their home in Wildwood, Illinois.

Stacey in Sedona, Arizona, in 2019, wearing a monarch and ready to take on the mission of helping bereaved children heal after the loss of a parent.

CPSIA information can be obtained
at www.ICGtesting.com
Printed in the USA
BVRC101437010322
630318BV00003B/93